Honore de Balzac

A Street of Paris and Its Inhabitant

Honore de Balzac

A Street of Paris and Its Inhabitant

1st Edition | ISBN: 978-3-73409-057-8

Place of Publication: Frankfurt am Main, Germany

Year of Publication: 2019

Outlook Verlag GmbH, Germany.

Reproduction of the original.

A STREET OF PARIS

AND

ITS INHABITANT

BY

HONORE DE BALZAC

Translated by

Henri Pene du Bois

Illustrated by

Francois Courboin

CONTENTS

PREPARER'S NOTE

This eBook was prepared from an edition published by Meyer Brothers and Company, New York, 1900.

Of this edition 400 copies were printed. 25 copies on Japan Paper, numbered 1 to 25. 375 copies on specially made paper, numbered 26 to 400.

PREFACE

This little Parisian silhouette in prose was written by Balzac to be the first chapter of a new series of the "Comedie Humaine" that he was preparing while the first was finishing. Balzac was never tired. He said that the men who were tired were those who rested and tried to work afterwards.

"A Street of Paris and its Inhabitant" was in its author's mind when Hetzel, engaged in collecting a copy for the work entitled "Le Diable a Paris" that all book lovers admire, asked Balzac for an unpublished manuscript.

Balzac gave him this, after retouching it, in order that it should have the air of a finished story. Why Hetzel did not use it in "Le Diable a Paris," no one knows. He went into exile, in Brussels, at the military revolution that made Napoleon III Emperor and, needing money, sold "A Street of Paris and its Inhabitant" with other manuscripts to Le Siecle.

Balzac's work was printed entire in three pages of the journal Le Siecle, in Paris, July 28, 1845. M. le Vicomte Spoelberch de Lovenjoul owns Balzac's autograph manuscript of it. These details are given by him and might be reproduced here with his signature. But the publishers wish not to be deprived of the pleasure of paying homage to the Vicomte Spoelberch de Lovenjoul.

He has made in the biography of Balzac, in editions of his books, in the pious collection of his unpublished writings, the ideal literary man's monument.

H. P. du B.

I

PHYSIOGNOMY OF THE STREET

Paris has curved streets, streets that are serpentine. It counts, perhaps, only the Rue Boudreau in the Chaussee d'Antin and the Rue Duguay-Trouin near the Luxembourg as streets shaped exactly like a T-square. The Rue Duguay-Trouin extends one of its two arms to the Rue d'Assas and the other to the Rue de Fleurus.

In 1827 the Rue Duguay-Trouin was paved neither on one side nor on the other; it was lighted neither at its angle nor at its ends. Perhaps it is not, even to-day, paved or lighted. In truth, this street has so few houses, or the houses are so modest, that one does not see them; the city's forgetfulness of them is explained, then, by their little importance.

Lack of solidity in the soil is a reason for that state of things. The street is situated on a point of the Catacombs so dangerous that a portion of the road disappeared recently, leaving an excavation to the astonished eyes of the scarce inhabitants of that corner of Paris.

A great clamor arose in the newspapers about it. The government corked up the "Fontis"—such is the name of that territorial bankruptcy—and the gardens that border the street, destitute of passers-by, were reassured the more easily because the tax list did not weigh on them.

The arm of the street that extends to the Rue de Fleurus is entirely occupied, at the left, by a wall on the top of which shine broken bottles and iron lances fixed in the plaster—a sort of warning to hands of lovers and of thieves.

In this wall is a door, the famous little garden door, so necessary to dramas and to novels, which is beginning to disappear from Paris.

This door, painted in dark green, having an invisible lock, and on which the tax collector had not yet painted a number; this wall, along which grow thistles and grass with beaded blades; this street, with furrows made by the wheels of wagons; other walls gray and crowned with foliage, are in harmony with the silence that reigns in the Luxembourg, in the convent of the Carmelites, in the gardens of the Rue de Fleurus.

If you went there, you would ask yourself, "Who can possibly live here?" Who? Wait and see.

II

SILHOUETTE OF THE INHABITANT

 One day, about three in the afternoon, that door was opened. Out of it came a little old man, fat, provided with an abdomen heavy and projecting which obliges him to make many sacrifices. He has to wear trousers excessively wide, not to be troubled in walking. He has renounced, long ago, the use of boots and trouser straps. He wears shoes. His shoes were hardly polished.

The waistcoat, incessantly impelled to the upper part of the gastric cavities by that great abdomen, and depressed by the weight of two thoracic bumps that would make the happiness of a thin woman, offers to the pleasantries of the passers-by a perfect resemblance to a napkin rolled on the knees of a guest absorbed in discussion at dessert.

The legs are thin, the arm is long, one of the hands is gloved only on most solemn occasions and the other hand ignores absolutely the advantage of a second skin.

That personage avoids the alms and the pity that his venerable green frock coat invites, by wearing the red ribbon at his button-hole. This proves the utility of the Order of the Legion of Honor which has been contested too much in the past ten years, the new Knights of the Order say.

The battered hat, in a constant state of horror in the places where a reddish fuzz endures, would not be picked up by a rag picker, if the little old man let it fall and left it at a street corner.

Too absent-minded to submit to the bother that the wearing of a wig entails, that man of science—he is a man of science—shows, when he makes a bow, a head that, viewed from the top, has the appearance of the Farnese Hercules's knee.

Above each ear, tufts of twisted white hair shine in the sun like the angry silken hairs of a boar at bay. The neck is athletic and recommends itself to the notice of caricaturists by an infinity of wrinkles, of furrows; by a dewlap faded but armed with darts in the fashion of thistles.

The constant state of the beard explains at once why the necktie, always crumpled and rolled by the gestures of a disquiet head, has its own beard, infinitely softer than that of the good old man, and formed of threads scratched from its unfortunate tissue.

Now, if you have divined the torso and the powerful back, you will know the sweet tempered face, somewhat pale, the blue ecstatic eyes and the inquisitive nose of that good old man, when you learn that, in the morning, wearing a silk head kerchief and tightened in a dressing-gown, the illustrious professor—he is a professor—resembled an old woman so much that a young man who came from the depths of Saxony, of Weimar, or of Prussia, expressly to see him, said to him, "Forgive me, Madame!" and withdrew.

This silhouette of one of the most learned and most venerated members of the Institute betrays so well enthusiasm for study and absent-mindedness caused by application to the quest of truth, that you must recognize in it the celebrated Professor Jean Nepomucene Apollodore Marmus de Saint-Leu, one of the most admirable men of genius of our time.

III

MADAME ADOLPHE

When the old man—the professor counted then sixty-two summers—had walked three steps, he turned his head at this question, hurled in an acute tone by a voice that he recognized:

"Have you a handkerchief?"

A woman stood on the step of the garden door and was watching her master with solicitude.

She seemed to be fifty years of age, and her dress indicated that she was one of those servants who are invested with full authority in household affairs.

She was darning stockings.

The man of science came back and said naively:

"Yes, Madame Adolphe, I have my handkerchief."

"Have you your spectacles?" she asked.

The man of science felt the side pocket of his waistcoat.

"I have them," he replied.

"Show them to me," she said. "Often you have only the case."

The professor took the case out of his pocket and showed the spectacles with a triumphant air.

"You would do well to keep them on your nose," she said.

M. de Saint-Leu put on his spectacles, after rubbing the glasses with his handkerchief.

Naturally, he thrust the handkerchief under his left arm while he set his spectacles on his nose. Then he walked a few steps towards the Rue de Fleurus and relaxed his hold on the handkerchief, which fell.

"I was sure of it," said Madame Adolphe to herself. She picked up the handkerchief and cried:

"Monsieur! Monsieur!"

"Well!" exclaimed the professor, made indignant by her watchfulness.

"I beg your pardon," he said, receiving the handkerchief.

"Have you any money?" asked Madame Adolphe with maternal solicitude.

"I need none," he replied naively, explaining thus the lives of all men of science.

"It depends," Madame Adolphe said. "If you go by way of the Pont des Arts you need one sou."

"You are right," replied the man of science, as if he were retracing instructions for a voyage to the North Pole. "I will go through the Luxembourg, the Rue de Seine, the Pont des Arts, the Louvre, the Rue du Coq, the Rue Croix-des-Petits-Champs, the Rue des Fosses- Montmartre. It is the shortest route to the Faubourg Poissonniere."

"It is three o'clock," Madame Adolphe said. "Your sister-in-law dines at six. You have three hours before you—Yes—you'll be there, but you'll be late." She searched her apron pocket for two sous, which she handed to the professor.

"Very well, then," she said to him. "Do not eat too much. You are not a glutton, but you think of other things. You are frugal, but you eat when you are absent-minded as if you had no bread at home. Take care not to make Madame Vernet, your sister-in-law, wait. If you make her wait, you will never be permitted again to go there alone, and it will be shameful for you."

Madame Adolphe returned to the threshold of the little door and from there watched her master. She had to cry to him, "To the right! To the right!" for he was turning toward the Rue Notre-Dame-des-Champs.

"And yet he is a man of science, people say," she muttered to herself. "How did he ever manage to get married? I'll ask Madame when I dress her hair."

IV

INCONVENIENCE OF QUAYS
WHERE ARE BOOK STALLS

At four o'clock, Professor Marmus was at the end of the Rue de Seine, under the arcades of the Institute. Those who know him will admit that he had done nobly, since he had taken only one hour to go through the Luxembourg and down the Rue de Seine.

There a lamentable voice, the voice of a child, plucked from the good man the two sous that Madame Adolphe had given to him. When he reached the Pont des Arts he remembered that he had to pay toll and turned back suddenly to beg for a sou from the child.

The little rascal had gone to break the coin, in order to give only one sou to his mother. She was walking up and down the Rue Mazarine with her baby at her breast.

It became necessary for the professor to turn his back on the veteran soldier who guards against the possibility of a Parisian passing over the bridge without paying the toll.

Two roads were open to him: the Pont Neuf and the Pont Royal. Curiosity makes one lose more time in Paris than anywhere else.

How may one walk without looking at those little oblong boxes, wide as the stones of the parapet, that all along the quays stimulate book lovers with posters saying, "Four Sous—Six Sous—Ten Sous—Twelve Sous—Thirty Sous?" These catacombs of glory have devoured many hours that belonged to the poets, to the philosophers and to the men of science of Paris.

Great is the number of ten-sous pieces spent in the four-sous stalls!

The professor saw a pamphlet by Vicq-d'Azyr, a complete Charles Bonnet in the edition of Fauche Borel, and an essay on Malus.

"And such then is the sum of our achievements," he said to himself. "Malus! A genius arrested in his course when he had almost captured the empire of light! But we have had Fresnel. Fresnel has done excellent things! —Oh, they will recognize some day that light is only a mode of substance."

The professor held the notice on Malus. He turned its pages. He had known Malus. He recalled to himself and recited the names of all the Maluses. Then he returned to Malus, to his dear Malus, for they had entered the Institute together at the return to Paris of the expedition to Egypt. Ah! It was then the Institute of France and not a mass of disunited Academies.

"The Emperor had preserved," said Marmus to himself, "the saintly idea of the Convention. I remember," he muttered aloud, "what he said to me when I was presented to him as a member of the Institute. Napoleon the First said, 'Marmus, I am the Emperor of the French, but you are the King of the infinitely little and you will organize them as I have organized the Empire.'

Ah, he was a very great man and a man of wit! The French appreciated this too late."

The professor replaced Malus and the essay on him in the ten-sous stall, without remarking how often hope had been lit and extinguished alternately in the gray eyes of an old woman seated on a stool in an angle of the quay.

"He was there," Marmus said, pointing to the Tuileries on the opposite bank of the river. "I saw him reviewing his sublime troops! I saw him thin, ardent as the sands of Egypt; but, as soon as he became Emperor, he grew fat and good-natured, for all fat men are excellent—this is why Sinard is thin, he is a gall-making machine. But would Napoleon have supported my theory?"

V

FIRST COURSE

It was the hour at which they went to the dinner table in the house of Marmus's sister-in-law. The professor walked slowly toward the Chamber of Deputies, asking himself if his theory might have had Napoleon's support. He could no longer judge Napoleon save from that point of view. Did Napoleon's genius coincide with that of Marmus in regard to the assimilation of things engendered by an attraction perpetual and continuous?

VI

SECOND COURSE

"No, Baron Sinard was a worshipper of power. He would have gone to the Emperor and told him that my theory was the inspiration of an atheist. And Napoleon, who has done a great deal of religious sermonizing for political reasons, would have persecuted me. He had no love for ideas. He was a courtier of facts! Moreover, in Napoleon's time, it would not have been possible for me to communicate freely with Germany. Would they have lent me their aid—Wytheimler, Grosthuys, Scheele, Stamback, Wagner?

"To make men of science agree—men of science agree!—the Emperor should have made peace; in time of peace, perhaps, he would have taken an interest in my quarrel with Sinard! Sinard, my friend, my pupil, become my antagonist, my enemy! He, a man of genius—

"Yes, he is a man of genius. I do justice to him in the face of all the world."

At this moment the professor could talk aloud without trouble to himself or to the passers-by. He was near the Chamber of Deputies, the session was closed, all Paris was at dinner—except the man of science.

Marmus was haranguing the statues which, it must be conceded, are similar to all audiences. In France there is not an audience that is not prohibited from giving marks of approval or disapproval. Otherwise, there is not an audience that would not turn orator.

At the Iena bridge Marmus had a pain in the stomach. He heard the hoarse voice of a cab driver. Marmus thought that he was ill and let himself be ushered into the cab. He made himself comfortable in it.

When the driver asked, "Where?" Marmus replied quietly:

"Home."

"Where is your home, Monsieur?" asked the driver.

"Number three," Marmus replied.

"What street?" asked the driver.

"Ah, you are right, my friend. But this is extraordinary," he said, taking the driver into his confidence. "I have been so busy comparing the hyoides and the caracoides—yes, that's it. I will catch Sinard in the act. At the next session of the Institute he will have to yield to evidence."

The driver wrapped his ragged cloak around him. Resignedly, he was saying to himself, "I have seen many odd folks, but this one—" He heard the word "Institute."

"The Institute, Monsieur?" he asked.

"Yes, my friend, the Institute," replied Marmus.

"Well he wears the red ribbon," said the driver to himself. "Perhaps he has something to do with the Institute."

The professor, infinitely more comfortable in his cab than on the sidewalk, devoted himself entirely to solving the problem that went against his theory and would not surrender—the rascal! The cab stops at the Institute; the janitor sees the Academician and bows to him respectfully. The cab driver, his suspicions dispelled, talks with the janitor of the Institute while the illustrious professor goes—at eight in the evening—to the Academie des Sciences.

The cab driver tells the janitor where he found his fare.

"At the Iena bridge," repeats the janitor. "M. Marmus was coming back from Passy. He had dined, doubtless, with M. Planchette, one of his friends of the Academy."

"He couldn't tell me his address," says the cab driver.

"He lives in the Rue Duguay-Trouin, Number three," says the janitor.

"What a neighborhood!" exclaims the driver.

"My friend," asks of the janitor the professor who had found the door shut, "is there no meeting of the Academy to-day?"

"To-day!" exclaims the janitor. "At this hour!"

"What is the time?" asks the man of science.

"About eight o'clock," the janitor replies.

"It is late," comments M. Marmus. "Take me home, driver."

The driver goes through the quays, the Rue du Bac, falls into a tangle of wagons, returns by the Rue de Grenelle, the Croix-Rouge, the Rue Cassette, then he makes a mistake. He tries to find the Rue d'Assas, in the Rue Honore-Chevalier, in the Rue Madame, in all the impossible streets and, swearing that if he had known he would not have come so far for a hundred sous, disembarks the professor in the Rue Duguay-Trouin.

The cab driver claims an hour, for the police ordinances, that defend consumers of time in cabs from the stratagems of cab drivers, had not yet posted the walls of Paris with their protecting articles that settle in advance all difficulties.

"Very well, my friend," says M. Marmus to the cab driver. "Pay him," M. Marmus says to Madame Adolphe. "I do not feel well, my child."

"Monsieur, what did I tell you?" she exclaimed. "You have eaten too much. While you were away, I said to myself, 'It is Mme. Vernet's birthday. They will urge him at table and he will come back sick.' Well, go to bed. I will make camomile tea for you."

VII

DESSERT

The professor walked through the garden into a pavilion at one of its corners, where he lived alone in order not to be disturbed by his wife.

He went up the stairway leading to his little room, and complained so much of his pains in the stomach that Madame Adolphe filled him with camomile tea.

"Ah, here is a carriage! It is Madame returning in great anxiety, I am sure," said Madame Adolphe, giving to the professor his sixth cup of camomile tea. "Now, sir, I hope that you will be able to drink it without me. Do not let it fall all over your bed. You know how Madame would laugh. You are very happy to have a little wife who is so amiable and so joyful."

"Say nothing to her, my child," exclaimed the professor, whose features expressed a sort of childish fear.

The truly great man is always more or less a child.

VIII

THIS SHOWS THAT THE WIFE OF
A MAN OF SCIENCE IS VERY UNHAPPY

"Well, good-bye. Return in the cab, it is paid for," Madame Marmus was saying when Madame Adolphe arrived at the door.

The cab had already turned the corner. Madame Adolphe, not having seen Madame Marmus's escort, said to herself:

"Poor Madame! He must be her nephew."

Madame Marmus, a little woman, lithe, graceful, mirthful, was divinely dressed and in a fashion too young for her age, counting her twenty-five years as a wife. Nevertheless, she wore well a gown with small pink stripes, a cape embroidered and edged with lace, boots pretty as the wings of a butterfly. She carried in her hand a pink hat with peach flowers.

"You see, Madame Adolphe," she said, "my hair is all uncurled. I told you that in this hot weather it should be dressed in bandeaux."

"Madame," the servant replied, "Monsieur is very sick. You let him eat too much."

"What could I do?" Madame Marmus replied. "He was at one end of the table and I at the other. He returned without me, as his habit is! Poor little man! I will go to him as soon as I change my dress."

Madame Adolphe returns to the pavilion to propose an emetic, and scolds the professor for not having returned with Madame Marmus.

"Since you wished to come in a cab, you might have spared me the expense of the one that Madame Marmus took. The charge for your cab was an hour. Did you stop anywhere?"

"At the Institute," he replied.

"At the Institute! Where did you take the cab?" she asked.

"In front of a bridge, I think," he replied.

"Was it still daylight?" she asked.

"Almost," he said.

"Then you did not go to Madame Vernet's!" exclaimed Madame Adolphe.

"Why did you not come to Madame Vernet's?" asked his wife.

Madame Marmus, having come to the door on the tips of her toes, had heard Madame Adolphe's exclamation. She did not wish to see Madame Adolphe's astonishment. Surely Madame Adolphe could not have forgotten the assurance with which the professor's wife had placed him in imagination at Madame Vernet's table.

"My dear child, I do not know," said the professor in a repentant tone.

"Then you have not dined," said Madame Marmus, whose attitude remained that of the purest innocence.

"With what could he have dined, Madame? He had two sous," said Madame Adolphe, looking at Madame Marmus with an accusing air.

"Ah, I am truly to be pitied, my poor Madame Adolphe," said Madame Marmus. "This sort of thing has been going on for twenty years, and I am not yet accustomed to it. Six days after our wedding, we were going out of our room one morning to take breakfast. M. Marmus hears the drum of the Polytechnic School pupils of whom he was the professor. He quits me to go and see them pass. I was nineteen years of age and when I pouted, you cannot guess what he said to me. He said, 'These young people are the flower and the glory of France!' This is how my marriage began. You can judge of the rest."

"Oh, Monsieur, is it possible?" asked Madame Adolphe with an indignant air.

"I have cornered Sinard!" exclaimed M. Marmus triumphantly.

"Oh, he would let himself die!" exclaimed Madame Adolphe.

"Get something for him to eat," said Madame Marmus. "He would let himself do anything. Ah, my good Madame Adolphe, a man of science, you see, is a man who knows nothing—of life."

The malady was cured by a cataplasm of Italian cheese that the man of science ate without knowing what he was eating, for he held Sinard in a corner—

"Poor Madame," said the kind Madame Adolphe. "I pity you. He was really so absent-minded as that!"

And Madame Adolphe forgot the strange avowal of her mistress.

Lightning Source UK Ltd.
Milton Keynes UK
UKHW041503130223
416650UK00010B/315